Flash
the
Firefly

written by Derrick Philip Begin

illustrated by Nguyen Thi Kieu Diem

Published in the United States by Begin Interactive

Printed by Lightning Source Inc., IngramSpark

ISBN-13: 978-0-9977372-0-2
ISBN-10: 0-9977372-0-4

10 9 8 7 6 5 4 3 2 1
First Edition – Hardcover

Visit us on the web at: www.flashfirefly.com

INTERACTIVE

www.begininteractive.com

For Jackson, Celia, and René the bright lights of my life.

Acknowledgments

Thank you to the following individuals and groups for their contributions, inspiration and knowledge in creating this book:

Emily for her encouragement and support.

Dad for taking us kids to a field with a couple of nail holed jam jars to catch fireflies.

YMCA Writer's Voice

Khac Art

Flash the Firefly lives in a field, near the city.

Flash is the brightest of all the fireflies.

In a blink his light makes the night disappear.

Night is Flash's favorite time. He frolics with his friends in the tall grass under the twinkling stars. FLASH!

There is Zig-Zag

who never flies straight.

Zippy is the fastest and little Blip.

Blip is the smallest firefly
having a very tiny light.

Blip is Flash's best friend.

Blip hopes to be like Flash one day.

Flash and his friends play games like

Hide and Seek,

　　Raindrop Dodge and

　　　Flash's much loved, "I'm Brightest!"

Flash is a very happy firefly.

This night is a very special night

because it's Flash's birthday!

The soft rain drizzled to a stop and
the dark clouds blew away.

Flash flew from under his green leaf.

FLASH!

He looked right, then left.

His friends were not around.

There were no other fireflies anywhere.

FLASH! FLASH! FLASH!

He called to them with his bright light.

No sight. No sound. Only the dark.

Where could

they have gone?

Flash flew through the air faster

than a gust of wind.

He looked in the old crab apple tree with the knot.

He blinked over Cat Tail Swamp.

He sailed over the field of sleeping cows, woolly sheep and wandering hens.

He was almost caught by
Craggy the fence spider's sticky web!
FLASH! FLASH! FLASH!

Flash landed on a blade of grass next to his green leaf home.

The glow from his light was fading fast.

He searched North, South, East and West,

everywhere a firefly could fly

and found no one.

What's being the brightest firefly

without having friends?

Flash missed his friends

especially his pal Blip.

His bright light began to sputter and dim.

The wind rustled

his leaf and swirled it

in circles carrying it

high above the trees

into the sky.

A crescent moon began to rise.

HAPPY

Flash looked up into the night and was surprised by a startling sight.

A spectacle of twinkling and flashing stars wrote in the sky:

BIRTHDAY

FLASH

HAPPY BIRTHDAY
FLASH!

They weren't stars at all.

His friends were _UP_ there!

All the fireflies including

Zig-Zag, Zippy and his best friend, Blip.

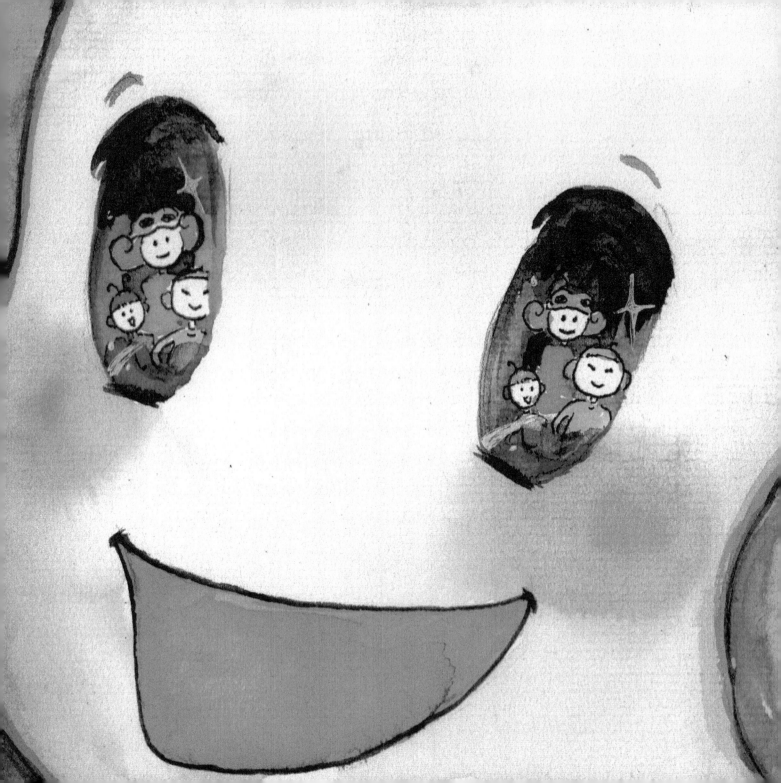

"Happy Birthday, Flash." Blip said as he swooped down to Flash's perch.

Flash was his bright and happy firefly self again.

FLASH! FLASH! FLASH!

About the Author

A native Mainer, Derrick grew up on the edge of an overgrown baseball field teeming with activity in Portland, Maine.

Since childhood, Derrick has been an avid reader and he loves to be in nature. His love of literature inspired him to write his own stories.

A graduate of University of Maine, Derrick makes his home in New York City with his wife and three children. He is an active member of Society of Children's Book Writers and Illustrators.